A Mother for the Chipmunks™

adapted by Megan Stine and H. William Stine

drawings by Neil Cole and Corne Cole
color by Cindy Lee

based on a story by Janice Karman and Ross Bagdasarian

Random House 🏠 New York

Copyright © 1985 Bagdasarian Productions. All rights reserved under International and Pan-American Copyright Conventions. Published in the United States by Random House, Inc., New York, and simultaneously in Canada by Random House of Canada Limited, Toronto.

Library of Congress Cataloging in Publication Data:
Stine, Megan. A mother for the Chipmunks. SUMMARY: The Chipmunks look for a wife for Dave so that they will have someone to take to the Mother and Son Picnic. 1. Children's stories, American. [1. Chipmunks—Fiction. 2. Humorous stories] I. Stine, H. William. II. Cole, Neil, ill. III. Karman, Janice. IV. Bagdasarian, Ross. V. Title. PZ7.S86035Mo 1985 [E] 84-18051 ISBN: 0-394-87150-2
Manufactured in the United States of America 1 2 3 4 5 6 7 8 9 0

THE CHIPMUNKS is a trademark of Bagdasarian Productions.

It was Friday afternoon—the best day of the week. Kids were leaving school in every direction. And everyone was looking forward to a great weekend—everyone except the three Chipmunks—Alvin, Simon, and Theodore.

"We've just got to face facts," Simon said. "Tomorrow is the school's annual Mother and Son Picnic. But we won't be going to it."

Just then Randy McTandy came by. Randy always looked for ways to be nasty—especially to the Chipmunks.

"Tomorrow's Mother and Son Picnic is going to be great. If you're lucky, I'll tell you guys all about it on Monday," Randy said to the Chipmunks with a mean smile. "Cheer up. Maybe next year they'll have an Orphans Picnic just so you guys can come."

Then Randy rode off on his bike, laughing as if he had just heard the funniest joke in the world.

"If they ever have a Mother and *Jerk* Picnic, you'll be the first one invited!" Alvin yelled after Randy.

"Who needs a mother anyway?" Theodore said, trying to sound brave. "She'd just make us pick up our toys and clean our room."

"That's right," Simon joined in. "And she'd boss us around all the time."

"And tuck us in at night," Alvin said.

"And make us snacks," Theodore said.

"And read to us," Simon said.

"And take us to the Mother and Son Picnic," Alvin added.

"I'd like a mother," Theodore said with a sad look in his eyes.

"But we don't have a mother," Simon said. "Only a father. And Dave will have to marry someone *tonight* if we want a mother to take us to the picnic tomorrow."

"But Dave's right in the middle of writing a new song," said Theodore. "He's too busy to find someone to marry tonight."

Suddenly Alvin's bicycle screeched to a stop. His eyes blinked twice and his mouth opened wide. Theodore and Simon knew what that look meant: Alvin was getting a brilliant idea.

"We need a mother to take us to the picnic, right? And Dave is too busy to find one, right?" Alvin said. "So we'll just have to find one for him!"

"Great!" Theodore and Simon shouted together.

But there was one big problem. Alvin, Simon, and Theodore each had a different idea about who would make a perfect mother. Alvin wanted her to be a great athlete. Simon wanted her to be super smart. And Theodore wanted her to be the world's greatest cook. Finally they agreed that there was only one fair and scientific way to find a mother.

"We'll each pick out a woman for Dave and we'll invite all three of them to come over tonight," Simon said. "Then Dave can choose the one he likes best."

Since it was Simon's idea, he got to go first. So Simon led his brothers to the Museum of Natural History. The museum was filled with hundreds of exhibits of rocks, fish, cave men, and enormous wild animals.

The Chipmunks looked through room after room until at last Simon found Dr. Meg Fleming. Dr. Fleming was a scientist who worked for the museum. She was busy trying to put the bones of a gigantic dinosaur skeleton together.

"That's an excellent example of Jurassic reptilian anatomy," Simon said, walking up to her.

Dr. Fleming turned around quickly. "Jurassic?" she asked.

"Clearly," Simon said.

"Aha! That's what I've been doing wrong," Dr. Fleming said. She quickly rearranged some of the bones until the dinosaur looked right. "Young man, you're remarkable. Where did you learn so much about dinosaurs?"

"I learned everything I know from my lonely, widowed father, Dr. David Seville," said Simon. "He wrote the famous book on the albino pterodactyl—and took the photos, too."

"How on earth did he get photos of an extinct dinosaur?" Dr. Fleming asked.

"Uh . . . I think he used a very old roll of film," Simon said. "He won't tell me all of his secrets because I'm not a scientist. But maybe he'll tell you."

"I'd like to talk to him sometime," Dr. Fleming said.

"How about tonight?" Simon blurted out. "Uh, I mean, you'd better hurry because he's leaving on an expedition tomorrow. He may not be back for years."

"Well, boys, I'd love to meet him," Dr. Fleming said. "But first I've got to finish putting this skeleton together."

"Here, let me help you," Theodore said, handing her a dinosaur bone. Unfortunately the bone was already attached—to another dinosaur.

After the crash Dr. Fleming scowled. "Tonight is out of the question!" she snapped. "I'll be here forever putting that brontosaurus back together again."

On their way out of the museum Theodore put his arm around Simon. "I'm sorry, Simon," Theodore said. "But Dave wouldn't have liked Dr. Fleming anyway. She was too skinny. There was no meat on her bones."

Now it was Theodore's turn to find the ideal mother. He headed straight for Ms. Crumm, the owner and chef of Crumm's Catering. As far as Theodore was concerned, anyone who could make perfect cookies, perfect cakes, and perfect pies would make a perfect mother for the Chipmunks.

The minute the Chipmunks entered Crumm's Catering shop, the smell of strawberry tarts overpowered them. But Theodore ignored it and got right down to business—the business of sampling the chocolate eclairs. He took a big bite and then began to choke.

Ms. Crumm came running out of the kitchen. "Jumping jelly rolls, child!" she said. "Are you trying to scare away my customers? What's wrong with you?"

"A dash too much salt in the pastry—maybe four or five grains," Theodore said, winking at his brothers.

Ms. Crumm quickly bit into one of the eclairs herself. Then her face turned bright red. "You're absolutely right, young man," she said. "I've made a big mistake. Where did you learn so much about cooking?"

"From my lonely, widowed father, Chef Pierre Seville. He was a master chef in Paris," Theodore said proudly. "He served so many fancy meals that he almost caused a butter shortage in France."

"Gracious gravy!" Ms. Crumm said. "I'd like to meet your father sometime."

"Well, he's cooking up a simple twelve-course snack tonight. Why don't you pop over?" Theodore said.

"Popovers? I almost forgot. I have to bake fifteen dozen popovers tonight for the Knights of Gooey Pastry's bake sale tomorrow," said Ms. Crumm. "I'll be up to my elbows in dough all night."

Theodore's face fell like a soufflé.

"We're running out of time," Alvin said to his brothers.

"And we're running out of perfect mothers, too," Theodore added.

So Alvin jumped on his bicycle and took off at top speed with Simon and Theodore close behind. They ended up in the sports arena, where the Worldwide Gymnastic Competition was being held.

Inside, the arena was packed with nervous athletes and excited fans. But one athlete stood out in the crowd. Not only did she win the most medals, but she won the most applause, too. She was Dana Beame, a young woman who had been a great gymnast ever since she was a little girl. Alvin was her number-one fan.

"Just think, you guys," Alvin said, watching Dana swing, bounce, and twist on the uneven parallel bars. "When Dana's our new mother, she can teach *us* to do that. I'll bet she could even teach Dave to roller-skate."

"I thought *you* were doing that by leaving your skates where he can trip over them," Simon said.

"Wish me luck, you guys," Alvin said. "This is our last chance to get a mother by tomorrow."

As soon as Dana finished her routine, Alvin rushed over to talk to her. "Nice dismount, Dana," Alvin said. "But you should try not to bend out of the double flip so soon. That's what my lonely, widowed father would say. He's been coaching ever since he won eighteen gold medals in the Olympic Games."

"Really? I'd like to meet—" Dana started to say.

But before she could finish the sentence, Morris Krasnakoff, her coach, came over. "Beat it, furball," Morris said to Alvin in a mean and grouchy voice.

"But we want to ask Dana to dinner tonight," Alvin said.

"Get out of here, before I go buy some mousetraps," Morris said, starting toward Alvin.

At that, Alvin took off running. He bounced onto the trampoline, which sent him flying toward the rings. He did a few triple flip-flops in the air and then sailed over toward the uneven bars. Three spins and a handstand later, Alvin landed back on his feet. The arena echoed with cheers as the crowd burst into applause.

Alvin took a bow. Then he took a look at Morris Krasnakoff, who had started after Alvin again. Without even waiting to see Alvin's score, the Chipmunks ran home in record time.

19

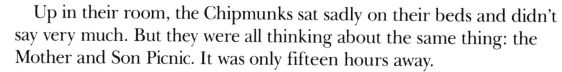

Up in their room, the Chipmunks sat sadly on their beds and didn't say very much. But they were all thinking about the same thing: the Mother and Son Picnic. It was only fifteen hours away.

"We need a mother," Theodore said sadly.

"Correction—we need a miracle," Simon said.

Suddenly the front doorbell rang. "I'll get it!" Dave shouted from downstairs.

The Chipmunks leaped off their beds and ran to the top of the stairs. They could see the front door open. Dr. Meg Fleming stood smiling at Dave.

"You must be Dr. David Seville," she said. "I'm Dr. Meg Fleming, and I hope I'm not too early for our date."

"Not too early for our *what*?" Dave asked.

"Our date," Dr. Fleming repeated. "I decided I couldn't pass up the opportunity to meet Simon's father—the man who wrote the famous book on the albino pterodactyl."

"Speaking of Simon," Dave said as he took Dr. Fleming into the den, "I think I'd better have a little talk with him. Excuse me, please."

But just as Dave was starting up the stairs, the doorbell rang again. Dave opened the door and there stood a woman in a bright flowered dress. She was holding a large layer cake that was decorated with flowers that matched her dress. It was Ms. Crumm.

"Good evening, Chef Seville. I brought dessert," Ms. Crumm said, marching straight into the kitchen.

"What are *you* doing here?" Dave asked as he followed her, completely confused.

"I was supposed to make popovers tonight, but I found some in the freezer," Ms. Crumm said. "Theodore is such a lucky boy to have a father like you."

The doorbell rang again. "Hi, I'm Dana Beame—" said the young woman at the door.

"Don't tell me—let me guess," Dave said. "Alvin invited you over to meet the world's greatest living skier, right?"

"You mean in addition to being an Olympic gold medal gymnast, you ski, too?" Dana said with surprise.

Dave politely asked Dana to wait in the living room. Then he headed directly for the Chipmunks' room upstairs. But he was too late. Alvin, Simon, and Theodore had already made their escape down the back stairs and out the back door.

"Now, remember, you guys," Simon said seriously. "We agreed to let Dave decide for himself which of the three women he wants to marry."

"Right," said Alvin. "But we didn't say anything about letting the *women* decide for themselves. I'm going to help them make up their minds!"

"Come back here!" Simon shouted.

"What are we waiting for?" Theodore said to Simon. "Let's go. It's every Chipmunk for himself!"

Alvin walked into the den on crutches and stopped in front of Dr. Fleming.

"Hi, I'm Alvin—Simon's brother," he said.

"Oh, were you in an accident?" Dr. Fleming said.

"It was my own fault," Alvin said. "I got a B-plus instead of an A on my report card. And Dave's got quite a temper if things don't go his way."

Dr. Fleming gasped. Alvin almost couldn't stop himself from laughing.

Outside the kitchen, Simon took off his glasses and then walked into the room, bumping into the walls and stepping on Ms. Crumm as he went.

"Whoops, sorry. I didn't know anyone was here," Simon said, blinking his eyes hard.

"Young man, you need glasses," Ms. Crumm said.

"I know," Simon said. "And I'm going to buy some. But first Dave— uh, Pierre—wants me to save up enough money to buy him a new car."

Ms. Crumm was so shocked that her face turned white.

Meanwhile, Theodore stepped into the living room with a duster and mop and smiled at Dana Beame. Suddenly he cried out, "Oh, no!"

"What's wrong?" Dana asked, almost vaulting out of her chair.

"Don't you see it? There's a teeny, tiny speck of dust on the table," Theodore said.

"I don't see anything," Dana said, bending over to look very closely at the table.

"I've been locked in the basement for a lot less than this," Theodore said.

Dana's jaw did a broad jump to the floor. "He locks you in the basement for dust?" she practically shouted.

"Yeah, but at least he doesn't chain me to the wall anymore," Theodore said.

"I'm getting out of here," Dana said. "I wouldn't go out with him if he were the last gold-medal winner on earth."

At the front door Dana ran into Ms. Crumm and Dr. Fleming.

"Who are *you*?" Dana asked them.

"I'm Mr. Seville's date," Dr. Fleming and Ms. Crumm said at the same time.

The women all glared at one another for a second. Then they glared at the Chipmunks. Then they glared at Dave when he came toward the door.

"There you guys are," Dave said sternly. "I want a word with you."

"Don't you touch them!" Dr. Fleming snapped. "These poor, sweet, innocent boys!"

"Making dates with three women for the same night—what an operator!" Dana snarled.

"I ought to give you a piece of my mind!" Ms. Crumm said. "But I think I'll just give you a piece of my cake instead."

With that, she smashed the whole four-layer cake into Dave's face and walked out the door. Dana Beame and Dr. Fleming followed right behind.

After the boys explained the whole story to Dave, he tucked them into bed.

"I'm sorry you're going to miss the Mother and Son Picnic tomorrow, guys. I know how badly you wanted to go. But finding someone to marry takes longer than one night. And it's something I've got to do by myself. Maybe next year."

"It's okay. Thanks for reading me the bedtime story, Dave," Simon said.

"Yeah. And thanks for bringing me the snacks, Dave," Theodore said.

"Yeah. And thanks for tucking me in, Dave," Alvin said.

"Well, good night, boys," Dave said, turning out the light.

"Isn't Dave a great mother?" Theodore said in the dark.

Suddenly the light clicked back on. Alvin's eyes blinked twice and his mouth fell open wide.

"He sure is a great mother!" Alvin said. "In fact, he's the best mother we could ever have. Let's take *him* to the Mother and Son Picnic."

And that's just what they did!

29